Within the fairy-tale treasury which has come into the world's possession, there is no doubt Hans Christian Andersen's stories are of outstanding character. Their symbolism is rich with character values. From his early childhood in the town of Odense, Denmark, until his death in Copenhagen, Hans Christian Andersen (1805-1875) wrote approximately 150 stories and tales. The thread in Andersen's stories is one of optimism which has given hope and inspiration to people all over the world. It is in this spirit that the Tales of Hans Christian Andersen are published.

WHAT THE OLD MAN DOES IS ALWAYS RIGHT

by Hans Christian Andersen

Translated from the original Danish text by Terence Andrew Day BA

Illustrated by Nathaele Vogel

U.S. edition 1988 by WORD Inc. Waco, TX 76702

Text: © Copyright 1987 Scandinavia Publishing House,
Nørregade 32, DK-1165, Copenhagen K, Denmark

Artwork: © Copyright 1987 Nathaele Vogel and
Scandinavia Publishing House

Printed in Denmark
by Aarhuus Stiftsbogtrykkerie

ISBN 0-8499-8542-0

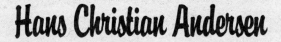

Hans Christian Andersen

What The Old Man Does
Is Always Right

Illustrated by Nathaele Vogel
Translated for children from the original Danish text
by Terence Andrew Day BA

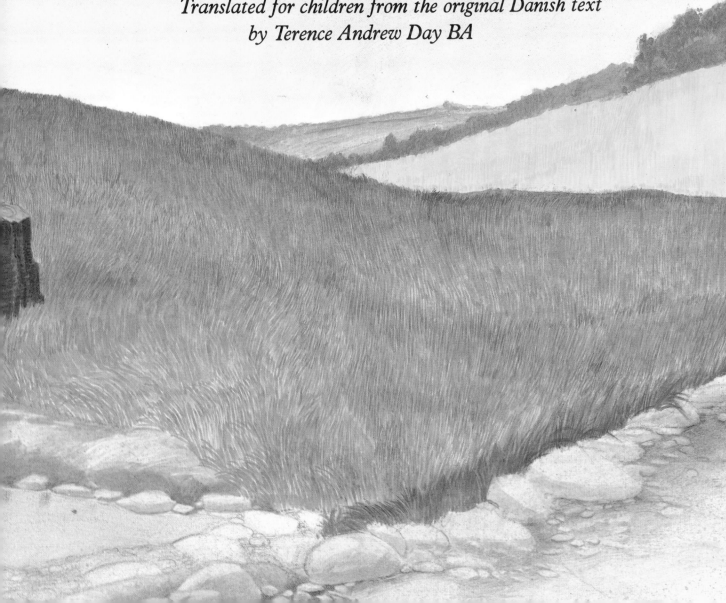

This is a story I heard when I was a little boy.

Every time I think about this story, it seems to become more and more charming. This is because stories are just like many people. They become more beautiful with age and that is a delightful thing!

Have you ever been out in the country? Then you've seen a proper old-fashioned farmhouse with a thatched roof, moss and lichen grow wild on the roof, and at the very top next to the chimney, there's a stork's nest. (We couldn't do without the good old stork, could we?)

The walls of the farmhouse are crooked. The windows, only one of which can be opened are just knee-high from the ground. Inside the house, the baking oven bulges out of the wall like a little fat belly.

Outside, the elderberry bush is hanging out over the hedge where there's a little pond. There the duck or ducklings swim right

underneath the gnarled old weeping-willow.
And don't forget the dog who barks at everyone
and anyone passing by.

Once upon a time, in just such a country
farmhouse as this lived two people, a farmer
and his wife. Although they did not own much,
there was one thing they could do without, and
that was their horse.

Their horse grazed along the ditch by the side
of the country lane. Sometimes the farmer rode
to town on it, the neighbors borrowed it and in
return, they would help him out. But sometimes
they wondered if it wouldn't be more useful to
sell the horse or exchange it for something,
rather than keep it. Which would it be?

"You'll know best, my old man!" said the
wife. "It's market day in town today, so you
ride into town, get some money for the horse or
make a good trade. Whatever you do is always
right! Yes, you go into town, my dear!"

Then she tied his scarf, for she could do it better than he, tying it with a double bow. And it did look charming. She brushed off his hat with the palm of her hand and kissed his warm lips, then off he rode on the horse which he was to sell or trade. Without a doubt, the old man knew what he was doing.

The sun was scorching hot, for there was not a cloud in the sky! The road was dusty, busy with so many people on their way to market, driving by carriage, riding on horseback and going on foot. It was a real heatwave with nowhere at all where you could find shade from the sun.

Along came a man driving a cow, as fine a cow as you ever have seen. "I bet that cow would give splendid milk!" thought the farmer. "That cow would be quite a good trade for my horse." "Hey, you there with the cow!" he said.

"How about us two having a little talk together? Now, a horse costs more than a cow, I would say, but I don't mind! A cow would be of better use to me. So what would you say to trading your cow for my horse?"

"It's a deal!" said the man with the cow. So they exchanged animals.

Once the farmer had his cow, he could just as well have gone back home. He had, after all, completed what he had set out to do.

But seeing as he had made up his mind to go to market, to market he would go. He just wanted to have a look, so off he went with his new cow.

He walked at a steady pace and so did the cow.
Before long they passed a man leading a sheep.
It was a fine sheep, well-fed and with a thick
woolly coat.

"I wouldn't mind having that!" thought the
farmer. "It would always have enough grass to
eat, grazing by our ditch. And in winter it could
stay inside the house with us. It would really be
more practical for us to keep a sheep than to
have a cow. Shall we swap?"

The man with the sheep agreed and so they
traded. And off went the farmer with his sheep
along the high road to market. A little further
on, he noticed a man carrying a large goose
under his arm.

"That's a heavy thing you've got there!" said the farmer. "It has plenty of feathers and plenty of fat! It would look fine waddling near our duck-pond and be just the right thing for the Missus for getting rid of all our scraps. She has often said, 'I wish we had a goose!' Well now she can have one. Yes, she shall have it! Do you want to trade? I'll give you my sheep for the goose and my thanks as well!"

The other man was glad to make the exchange and so they swapped; the farmer was given the goose.

By now he was near the town and the road became busier and busier. There was a rushing and bustling of people and animals alike. They were walking along the path and across the ditch leading into the toll-keeper's potato fields. The toll-keeper's hen stood tied to the gate there, so that it would not get frightened by the crowds, wander off and get lost.

The hen had short tailfeathers, winked with the one eye and looked very fine indeed. "Cluck, cluck!" it said. What it meant by that I do not know. But as the farmer watched the bird he thought, "she's the finest hen I have ever seen. She's finer than our parson's prize broodhen. I would like to have that hen! A hen can always find grain by itself and doesn't need much looking after, I think it would be a good exchange if I swapped it for the goose."

"Shall we trade?" he asked. "Trade?" said the other man. "Yes, that wouldn't be a bad idea!" And so they swapped. The toll-keeper took the goose and the farmer took the hen.

16

Now he had certainly done a great deal of business on this trip to town. By now he was quite tired and it was still hot. A good drink of ale and a bite to eat was just what he needed. He was about to enter the inn when the innkeeper came out. He met him at the door, carrying a sack.

"What have you got there?" asked the farmer.

"Rotten apples!" answered the innkeeper, "a whole sackful for my pigs."

"That's an awful amount to be throwing away like that! I wish my Missus could see all of them. Last year we only got one apple from the old tree by the manure heap! So we put it away safe on top of our chest of drawers until it went rotten and burst. "It's always wealth!" as our Missus would say. Here she could really see wealth! Yes, I wish she could see this."

"Well, what will you give me for them?" said the innkeeper.

"Give you? I know what, you can have my hen in exchange!" So he swapped his hen for the apples and went inside the inn, over to the bar.

19

He placed the sackful of apples right next to the stove which had just been heated up, without giving it a thought.

There were many guests in the room, horse-dealers, cattle-traders and two Englishmen who were so rich, their pockets were bursting at the seams with gold coins. Now they were fond of making bets, as you shall hear!

"Hiss-s-s! Hiss-ss!" What was that noise coming from the stove? It was the apples beginning to roast!

"What's that?" asked one of the Englishmen. Well it did not take long before they were told the whole story about the horse that was traded for a cow, and how finally the farmer had ended up with a sackful of rotten apples.

"Well, well, you'll be in big trouble with the Missus when you get home!" said the Englishmen, "What yelling there'll be in that house!"

"She'll give me a kiss and won't be mad at all!" said the farmer. "Our Missus will say,'what my old man does is always right!' "

"Shall we have a bet?" the Englishmen said. "We'll bet a barrel of gold coins, that is a hundred pounds in weight!"

"I'll make do with a bushel full, if you please!" said the farmer, "I can only bet a bushel full of apples and throw myself and the Missus into the bargain. But that's more than just a fair deal, that's real generous of me!"

"All right, you're on!" they said, and the bet was made.

The innkeeper's carriage was brought to the door. The Englishmen got in, together with the farmer and his rotten apples, and they went to the farmer's house.

"Good evening, Missus!"

"Thank you, my dear old man!"

"I've done my swap!"

"You know what you're doing!" said the wife. And she gave him a big hug, forgetting all about the sack and the strangers.

"I've traded the horse for a cow!"

"Heaven be praised for the milk!" said the wife. "Now we'll have plenty of milk, butter and cheese on the table. That was a good exchange!"

"Yes, but then I swapped the cow for a sheep!"

"Why, that's even better!" said the wife, "You always think of everything. We've got just enough grazing ground for a sheep. Now we can have sheep's milk and cheese and woollen stockings, yes, and even woollen jumpers!"

"A cow couldn't do that! Cows lose their hair! You're such a thoughtful man!"

"But I swapped the sheep for a goose!"

"So we'll have roast goose this year for Christmas, old man! You always know how to make me happy! That was so thoughtful of you! We can keep the goose out in the yard and it can grow fatter until Christmas!"

"But I swapped the goose for a hen!" said the farmer.

"A hen! that was a good trade, dear," said the wife, "Hens lay eggs, and when they hatch we'll have chicklings and our own chicken yard! That's just what I wanted!"

"Yes, but I traded the hen for a sackful of rotten apples!"

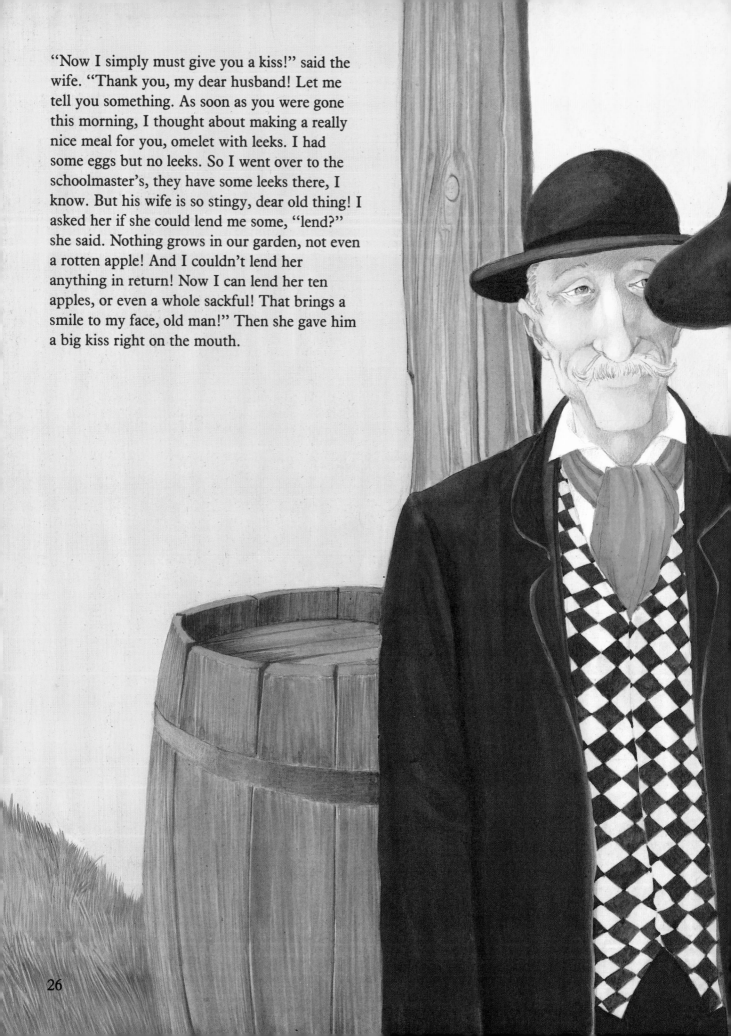

"Now I simply must give you a kiss!" said the wife. "Thank you, my dear husband! Let me tell you something. As soon as you were gone this morning, I thought about making a really nice meal for you, omelet with leeks. I had some eggs but no leeks. So I went over to the schoolmaster's, they have some leeks there, I know. But his wife is so stingy, dear old thing! I asked her if she could lend me some, "lend?" she said. Nothing grows in our garden, not even a rotten apple! And I couldn't lend her anything in return! Now I can lend her ten apples, or even a whole sackful! That brings a smile to my face, old man!" Then she gave him a big kiss right on the mouth.

26

"That's what I like to see!" said the Englishmen. "Always going downhill and always just as happy! That's worth paying money for!" So they paid the farmer a hundred pounds in gold coins because his wife gave him a kiss and not a scolding.

Well, there you are, it's always worthwhile for the wife to realize and tell others that her old man's the wisest, and no matter what he does, he is always right.

That was a story I heard when I was a little boy, and now you have heard it too, and know that the old man is always right.

Explaining the story:

Every person has strengths and weaknesses. The farmer and his wife lived simple, carefree lives and always saw the best in what happened around them. Instead of nagging and complaining, they treated each other with respect and trust. These were their strengths. On the other hand, the farmer and his wife seem to be a bit too simple. They did not use wisdom to help balance the good in their lives. That they were sometimes foolish was their weakness.

Talking about the truth of the story:

1. Why was the farmer still successful, even though he did not make very wise business choices?

2. Wisdom means common sense coupled with good judgment. What might have happened in the story if the farmer had practiced wisdom?

3. What is the difference between wisdom and knowledge?

Applying the truth of the story:

1. Name someone you would describe as wise. Why?

2. How can you learn to become wise?